CW0085871B

A MESSAGE FROM CHICKEN HOUSE

Pudding's back! Everyone's favourite panda has to wrestle with her own ego when a pushy journalist tempts her with fame and fortune . . . Luckily, Callum's on the case, determined to prove the journalist is up to something very fishy indeed. You'll fall head over heels for Sarah Horne's charming and hilarious illustrations in this fantastic follow-up to *Panda at the Door*. Move over, Paddington – there's a new bear on the block!

BARRY CUNNINGHAM
Publisher
Chicken House

PANDA
IN THE
SPOTLIGHT

Written by Emma Read
with Sarah Horne

2 PALMER STREET, FROME,
SOMERSET BA11 1DS

First published in Great Britain in 2022
Chicken House
2 Palmer Street
Frome, Somerset BA11 1DS
United Kingdom
www.chickenhousebooks.com

Chicken House/Scholastic Ireland, 89E Lagan Road, Dublin Industrial Estate,
Glasnevin, Dublin D11 HP5F, Republic of Ireland

Cover and interior design and typesetting by Steve Wells
Printed and bound in Great Britain by CPI Group (UK) Ltd, Croydon CR0 4YY

FSC
www.fsc.org
MIX
Paper from
responsible sources
FSC® C171272

1 3 5 7 9 10 8 6 4 2

British Library Cataloguing in Publication data available.

ISBN 978-1-913696-24-5
eISBN 978-1-913696-62-7

For Pops

CHAPTER 1
Putting on a Show

P udding beamed from ear to furry ear as she stood in the white glow of the spotlight and took a bow. She let the applause from the audience pour over her like a warm and friendly breeze. This was Pudding's favourite part of the show – it reminded her of her days as Edinburgh Zoo's Star Attraction, where she was surrounded, day after day, by smiling faces and happy children. It filled her with the most delightful feeling – sweet, just like a spoonful of sugar. She looked to her co-star, Graham, who was smiling beside her.

They rose up and Graham gave her the merest nod. This was her next cue. Graham opened his arms as wide as he could and rushed forward for the biggest hug he could manage. As planned, he bounced off her fluffy tummy and fell on to the stage, on his bottom. The audience roared and Graham chuckled to himself, as he did every performance. Despite an increasingly bruised backside, the joke never got old for him.

Pudding scanned the crowd again, delighted at the sea of

happy faces, but then her eyes caught on a sharp-faced blonde woman near the front. Unlike everyone else, *she* wasn't smiling. Poor lady – Pudding wished she could wrap her in a big panda hug to cheer her up.

They took their final bow and exited stage left, as the clapping continued. Graham grinned at Pudding. 'Another encore, pet?'

'Not this time. First rule of showbiz: always leave them wanting more,' Pudding advised.

Back in the dressing room, Graham

grabbed a bottle of water and collapsed on to the battered old sofa. It was their second performance of the day – the theatre bosses had requested an extra matinee, because the show was so popular.

'Just gonnae close ma eyes for a moment, I'm knackered,' he said.

As Graham rested a lavender eye-mask over his face, there was a loud knock at the door.

'Excuse me, Graham and Pudding – there's a reporter to see you. From the *Edinburgh Tattle*. Penelope . . . something.' The stage manager sounded rattled. 'She's asking for an interview.'

'Och, you know we don't give interviews,' Graham said, removing the lavender eye-mask and sitting up.

Pudding peered round him into the corridor, where she recognized the sad woman from the audience, typing something on her phone with a frown. Now was her chance to cheer the poor mite up! She hated to see anyone leave the show unhappy. Pudding poked Graham in the arm.

'Ow!'

She stuck a clawed thumbs-up in front of his face and nodded furiously.

'Sorry, this reporter's very persistent,' the young man said, pushing his glasses up his nose as he glanced between Pudding and Graham. Like everyone else, he assumed Pudding was an actor in a panda suit. It was for the best – if anyone found out she was a real talking panda, let alone one who had escaped from the zoo a year ago, they'd be in big trouble – but it did mean Pudding had to keep schtum in front of anyone outside the family. 'Shall I tell her it's a no?'

Pudding shook her head at Graham sternly and thumbs-upped a second time. He blew a long breath out of his lips. 'That's all right,' he said begrudgingly. 'We'll see her for a quick natter. Just . . . give us a couple of minutes, OK?'

'What are you playing at, Pud?' Graham said when the stage manager had left. 'Ye ken this is risky to say the least!'

'The journalist – she's really sad, Graham. I saw

her in the crowd. She wasn't even laughing! This interview should make her smile.' Pudding smiled broadly at Graham and his expression softened. 'I promise I'll keep quiet, OK?'

'All right, pet. You've a kind heart, you know that?'

'Doesn't mean I won't enjoy the interview too!' Pudding swirled a pink feather boa around her shoulders. 'I'm ready for my close-up!'

Graham chuckled. 'Watch it – the fame might go to your head! We'd best be careful, though. It's one thing for you to pretend to be a person in a panda suit on stage, but close up . . . I wonder if we should glue buttons on to your fur – make it look more like a costume.'

But there was a knock on the door, and before Graham could stop her, Pudding sang, 'Come in!' before slapping a paw over her mouth in horror.

The door opened and the sad lady from the audience peered into the dressing room.

Graham cleared his throat. 'Sorry, hen. Do come in. Had a bit of a frog in my throat there,' he said gruffly.

The journalist was exactly as Pudding imagined a glamorous journalist should be. She had long smooth blonde hair, perfect make-up, a neat suit and a designer handbag.

Graham shook her hand enthusiastically. 'Pleasure to meet ye,

Penelope. I'm—'

'It's Penni, actually. Penni P,' the reporter interrupted. She reached a hand out cautiously, towards Pudding. 'And who are you? Really?'

'She's Pudding,' Graham said quickly, shooting Pudding a warning glance.

Penni reached into her handbag for a small leather notebook and offered Pudding a measured stare. Pudding nodded and smiled, holding her tongue. She suddenly felt a little deflated. Penni hadn't even said thank you for the interview – and she didn't appear to have cheered up at all!

Penni forced a tight-lipped smile and turned to Graham. 'So, Mr Campbell, how did you think up the idea for *Panda-mime*?'

Pudding and the Campbells had a ready-prepared story for the inspiration behind their sell-out show. Obviously, they couldn't very well tell the world it was easy to create such a panda-tastic work of genius when half of the act was, in fact, a *real* panda.

'Well, actually, it was my daughter Tabitha who started it all. She absolutely loves pandas, has them all over her bedroom – panda pyjamas, bedcovers, snow globes . . .' Graham pulled his phone out of his pocket. 'Here, I've got some great pictures.'

Graham scrolled through photos of his children without noticing that Penni was looking everywhere but at his phone.

'May I take a look at the costume?' Penni said abruptly.

'Well—'

But Penni P had already walked over to Pudding and looked her up and down, then round and round, like everyone always did – searching for the zip or buttons in the costume. Despite her good intentions towards the woman, Pudding felt herself bristle slightly. How rude!

'Perhaps if you told me who's inside the suit, my paper would print an exclusive story – it might

even end up on the front pages, who knows? Great publicity for you.'

'We'd never reveal that, I'm afraid,' said Graham. 'The mystery guest on stage is absolutely top secret.'

Penni tapped her pen against her lips. 'What about if I guess, and you say "yes" if I'm right? Apparently Jodie Whittaker bought a holiday home in the area recently. Have you got Doctor Who in there?' She stroked Pudding's arm and Pudding felt her fingers sinking into her soft, warm fur. 'So realistic.'

Pudding didn't care for being prodded and poked. She stretched out a paw and gently ruffled Penni P's hair until it stood up on end – see how she liked it! That stopped the reporter in her tracks. She pulled away and turned towards the Hollywood mirror to smooth down her no-longer-perfect hair.

Pudding loved her dressing room – the lights on the mirror made her feel like a real star, as did the hatstand in the corner, which was draped with colourful scarves, boas and beads. There was *Mary Poppins* memorabilia everywhere, from little dolls, to kites, to a signed photo of Dick Van Dyke and the penguins. The table itself was barely visible under cards and drawings from fans and well-wishers, and tucked in the corner of the mirror was a photo of Gerald, Pudding's former zookeeper friend at Edinburgh Zoo. Next to her fur-brushes and fur-spray was a large glass of water filled with juicy bamboo stalks. Pudding licked her lips.

Graham gave a little cough. 'So, Miss, er, P? What else can we tell you about the show? Or have you got everything you need?'

Penni seemed distracted, more like she was doing complicated maths in her head, rather than fixing her hair. She stared at the photo of Gerald, and the bamboo and the picture of Mary Poppins with a small cut-out of Pudding's face in place of Julie Andrews, as if that were more interesting than the giant panda sat beside her.

Pudding began to worry that they weren't going to get a good review and that perhaps she should start singing or juggling, when suddenly Penni appeared to figure out whatever it was that was bothering her, and her face transformed. She smiled a big, flashy, toothy smile, just like all the children used to at the zoo, whenever a grown-up with a camera phone mentioned 'cheese'. When she smiled like that, Penni P was radiant and sparkly. Pudding's heart felt warm; they really *had* cheered her up.

Penni P turned back to face them, crossing her legs and leaning closer to Graham.

Resting her notepad on her knee, pen poised, she said, 'Call me Penni, please. And tell me everything, Graham. And I mean, *everything*.' She paused. 'And then I might have some exciting news for you.'

CHAPTER 2
What Callum Heard

As Callum climbed the stairs to Pudding's dressing room, he wondered why people always said 'break a leg' to actors. It was supposed to be good luck, but he was pretty sure that was exactly what was about to happen to him, as he struggled to see over the jungle of bouquets in his arms. It didn't feel especially lucky.

Then he checked himself. Actually, he *should* feel lucky – ever since *Panda-mime* had brought down the

house at the Edinburgh Fringe festival, and they'd moved to their regular spot at the Roar Theatre, tickets had been selling like hot cakes. Or *panda cakes*, thought Callum, and his tummy rumbled.

Once Pudding came to live with them, panda cakes had been Cal and his sister Tabby's highlight of the week. Normal pancakes were OK, but panda cakes, well, they were fat and fluffy and practically perfect, especially when smothered in a generous layer of chocolate spread. Once Pudding had got the hang of leaving out the eggshells, that was.

Yes, they were very lucky to have Pudding – even though technically it wasn't luck. Callum's parents had adopted her from the zoo for Callum's birthday last year – except, they'd got a bit more than they bargained for when an actual

panda turned up on the doorstep, claiming to be a live-in nanny. But although it had been strange at first, Pudding had turned out to be the best nanny ever . . . not that he needed one, of course, he was too old for that sort of thing. No, she wasn't a glorified babysitter, she was more like – Cal spotted the latest *Panda-mime* poster with Pudding's big beaming face almost bursting out of it – like a friend.

And now the 'bacon' (which Cal knew was adult-speak for money) was rolling in, life was so much better!

As he reached the first floor, Cal heard muffled voices coming from the star of the show's dressing room, on the floor above.

They must still be talking to that reporter from the Edinburgh Tattle *the stage manager told me about,* he thought. Which was weird, because they had agreed they wouldn't do interviews.

It sounded like it was going well though, so he decided not to interrupt. If they got a good review in the *Tattle* they'd be properly set. Maybe they could even move to a bigger house – somewhere away from his neighbour Mike Spiker and his mean comments. Even though life was better, the Spikers still hung around like a bad smell.

Cal pushed the thought to one side and tried to concentrate on keeping the huge petals of the flowers out of his face. He didn't normally have hay fever, but with this much pollen flying about in his face, his nose was starting to tingle.

Just around the corner was a small alcove with a little sitting area, where there used to be an old-fashioned phone on the wall. Callum laid the flowers on the seat and exhaled with relief as he sat down.

His bottom had barely hit the upholstery when he realized he could see a reflection of Pudding's dressing room door in the very top of a tall mirror opposite the seat. And the door was opening.

The reporter from the *Tattle* emerged from the dressing room and headed his way. Cal studied her face as she descended the stairs, trying to work out if it had gone well, but her expression was difficult to read. She looked like she'd eaten something disgusting and was looking for someone to complain to. But at the same time she sort of looked happy about it. She rummaged in her handbag for her mobile phone. Callum watched as she tapped the screen frantically, then cast a sneaky glance back at Pudding's closed door. She looked weird – fidgety,

like she couldn't make her fingers work quickly
enough. It probably didn't help that she was gripping
a fat piece of bamboo in her fist.

From his seat in the snug, Callum didn't think
she could see him, and something about her manner
made him not want to change that.

She raised the phone to her ear and looked again
at Pudding's door, and then up and down the stairs.
It was all very suspicious. The sneeze prickled
a bit more insistently
and Callum silently
squeezed his nose.

'Amber, it's me.
Can you talk?'
The reporter
spoke quietly
but urgently.
There was a

pause and then, 'Yes, I've just been to that panda show I got the tip-off about.' Another pause. 'Of course, it was terrible – pun after pun, and all the falling over, ugh, excruciating. I mean, I know it's a sell-out, but there's no accounting for taste.'

There was a pause and Cal assumed the person on the other end of the phone was telling her how wrong she was and that *Panda-mime* was the best show ever. He had to bite his cheek to resist leaping up to defend Pudding and Dad as her complaints continued. OK, Dad's puns *were* a bit corny, but they were funny too. How dare she? Wasn't she supposed to be saying nice things about the show? He let out a little snort which rustled the plastic wrapping around the flowers.

The reporter stopped talking and her eyes darted about, hunting for the source of the sound. Cal held his breath.

She apparently decided she'd imagined it, and continued, a sneer growing on her face. 'Anyway, it was all worth it. Everyone at the *Tattle* will be queuing up for my stories once I've finished here. That tip-off was spot on: I've just got the scoop of the year.'

Cal squinted. One minute she's saying Dad's extra-cruciating and the next that *Panda-mime* is a scoop? It didn't make sense.

'I can't say too much, but the whole thing is a con! That panda isn't what it seems . . . no – that's just the thing, it's not a fancy costume. In fact, it's not a costume at all!'

Cal's eyes went as wide as the sunflowers on the seat beside him. *Oh no!*

'I don't have any proof yet . . .' She tucked the bamboo in her bag. 'But I know that Graham Campbell is lying and I am going to get to the bottom of it.

He didn't count on Penni P's investigative skills.'
Penni paused again. 'Penni P!' she snapped. 'It's my
journalist name. Anyway, that doesn't matter. What

does is that I know what's really going on behind the scenes of this so-called "hilarious" show, and now all I have to do is prove it.'

Cal's blood began to boil, his heart beat faster and his nose twitched even more urgently.

'I'd better go. I can't stand to hang around in this dive for much longer.'

It was no good. The combination of pollen and fury were too much. Callum managed to contain the noise as much as he could, and sneeze-snorted into his hand. Penni P froze again and looked behind her, but from where she was standing she couldn't see the little alcove where Callum was hiding.

'Sorry, Amber, I missed what you just said . . . Oh, yes, I'll get milk on the way home.' She took another baffled look around, and stalked away, down the corridor.

CHAPTER 3
La-La-La

'Cal? Is that you in there, pet?' Pudding peered through the bouquet blocking her dressing-room door. She parted the peonies and sunflowers, and sure enough, there was Callum Campbell, looking redder than the roses.

He bundled the bouquets into her arms and pushed past into the room.

'Dad! Pud! What happened? How did she find out? What are we going to do . . . Dad?'

Graham, looking calm and rather pleased with himself, helped Pudding with the flowers. 'Cal? Are you feeling quite all right? We've got the most amazing news. I think you need to sit down.'

Huh?

Cal looked at Pudding – she had the same dreamy look on her face as his dad. 'No! *You* need to sit down. I know what happened. But don't worry, I'm not going to let her get away with it.'

'What are you talking about, Cal? Get away with what? Who?'

Cal ran his hands through his hair. 'Penni P. She's on to us. I heard everything.'

Pudding gave him a big squeeze. 'Well, yes – she most certainly is on to us. And it's wonderful. We're going to be famous. More famous than we already are! Hollywood, here we come!'

Graham sat Cal down and told him everything

that Penni P had said to them. It was quite a different story than the one Cal had heard moments earlier. His dad's version of the meeting was all about Penni's superstar movie producer friend in Los Angeles who wanted to meet them. Apparently, it was the *Mary Poppins* merchandise that had given her the idea – Penni's friend, Amber, just happened to be starting work on a new Mary Poppins movie and they were looking for a new star to play Mary Poppins. Penni was confident that Pudding would be perfect – why not a panda nanny? And Graham too, for the role of Bert – Mary's chimney sweep friend.

'We're going to America, sweetheart,' said Graham, grabbing Cal by the shoulders.

Cal put his head in his hands. 'No, no, no. She's tricking you. I heard her on the phone outside. She said you were excretory or something and that it was a con and she was going to prove it. She knows that you're a *real* panda, Pudding.'

Dad just smiled. 'You've got quite an imagination, Cal! No, she thinks Pudding is someone in a furry suit. Come on, love. Mum will be waiting to drive us all home.'

The more Callum protested, the more Dad and Pudding refused to listen. Instead, they told him how the reporter had tried to guess the identity of the person in the panda suit.

'When she suggested I was Lady Gaga – that was the best!' Pudding clasped her hands to her heart.

'And then the Queen.' Graham chuckled. 'We've been there before!'

But Cal couldn't even bring himself to giggle at the memory of Pudding fooling Spiker's dad into thinking she was the actual Queen. No, all Cal could do was follow them to the car, frowning and trying to work out how to get them to believe him. Because if he didn't, their whole world was about to come crashing down.

At home, things got even worse.

Once Dad and Pudding had told Mum and Tabby their amazing 'news', everyone in the Campbell house went suddenly, and completely, mad.

Although Callum was a different kind of mad to the rest of them.

Tabby was the worst. The instant Pudding had told them about Penni P's friend, A-list Amber, Tabby had put on *The Greatest Showman* album and hadn't stopped singing since.

She was annoying on a good day, and today was definitely not a good day.

Cal left them to it, and sat on the front step.

Had he got it so wrong? He tried playing Penni P's phone conversation back in his head, but though his memory had gone a bit fuzzy on the details he knew she was definitely mean about the show. And she definitely had said Pudding wasn't in a panda costume. They didn't need to know any more than that!

Cal beat his fist against the wall.

'Oi, Campbell. Ye wannae fight somethin' that fights back, ye scaredy cat.'

Mike Spiker, from across the road.

Cal kept his head down. Mike had never forgiven him for the humiliating incident when his dad, Spud Spiker, had been fooled into thinking Pudding was the Queen when Mike had told him she was a panda.

"Ere, has your

dad actually told a funny joke yet? Och, that's right, I forgot – YOU'RE the family joke.' He booted his football against the wall, millimetres from Cal's face. 'Well, none of youse are gonnae be laughing soon.' He gave Cal a trademark sneer and dribbled his ball up the street, laughing as he went.

What did he mean by that? Callum wondered.

He went indoors and tried to slink up to his bedroom – but Pudding emerged from the living room and stopped him on the stairs. She was wearing leg warmers and star-shaped sunglasses.

'Callum? Are you all right?' she said. 'You should be celebrating with the rest of us!'

'I'm not in the mood. You didn't hear what I heard,' he mumbled. 'I don't trust Penni P. Not one bit.'

Pudding's face softened and she climbed up to sit by Callum on the steps. Her bottom was so big and

fluffy, he had to squeeze right up to the banisters –
but he didn't mind.

'I know your heart's in the right place, Callum,'
she said softly, 'but this is the real deal. All my dreams

are coming true! I'm really going to be Mary Poppins. I'm really going to be famous!' Her eyes were moist as she peered at the stars through the little window above the front door. Then she gazed down at Callum, placing a big furry arm around his shoulders. 'Are you, maybe, a little bit afraid of everything changing? Perhaps you think you're going to lose me and your dad to Hollywood, hmm?'

That wasn't it – but Callum didn't deny it. He just shrugged. He could tell there was no point in arguing: Pudding wanted the good news to be true so much that she wouldn't listen.

'It's all right, Callum. You don't need to be afraid. Whatever happens, we're family now.' Pudding hugged him close and in spite of everything, he really did feel a little bit better. Panda hugs were good for everything.

'Thanks,' Callum mumbled.

When Pudding had gone back to dancing in the living room, Callum lay down on his bed and tried to muffle the party noise by burying his head under his pillows. He was sure Penni was lying about the Mary Poppins movie. But how could he convince a family that had gone LA loopy, before it was too late?

With cold, hard evidence, he thought, as he drifted off to sleep.

CHAPTER 4
A Musical Interlude

The next morning, Cal woke to a horrendous noise outside his window.

It was a thunderous thumping, and somewhere underneath it all was music.

Don't tell me they're still at it, thought Cal.

He had hoped that the excitement would've died down by now and he could speak to the family sensibly.

It was not to be.

As he pulled back the curtains, it took him a

moment to realize what he was seeing. Pudding was wearing what looked like a partially fastened wedding dress with a red sash and a matching wide-brimmed straw hat. She was carrying one of the family umbrellas – a battered spotty one with one broken spoke. Dad was in a red-and-white striped blazer. They were arm in arm, skipping along the driveway and singing something about jolly holidays.

What on *earth* were they doing?

Dad grabbed Pudding's arm and launched her on to the bonnet of their car, where she sat gracefully.

There was a painful sound of groaning metal, then Pudding leapt on to the pavement, her white dress flapping out behind her. Callum could see she'd left a large dent on the driver's side.

Perhaps it was all just a terrible dream and if he went back to bed it would all be over. As he drew the curtains closed again, he saw the other residents of

Bumblescrape Street beginning to open their doors and peer outside – the Spikers included. Callum watched with cold dread as Mike Spiker sniggered. Then he remembered Mike's strange comment – *'None of youse are gonnae be laughing soon.'*

Did he have something to do with the arrival of Penni P?

*

'Sorry about the car, Graham,' said Pudding, once they'd all come inside.

'No matter, hen.' Graham shrugged. 'Once we've made a fortune we'll buy a new one.'

Mum gave Graham a half-convinced look and Pudding was worried. What if Mum didn't want to come? She was definitely the sensible half of the couple. Then she noticed that she was looking at 'homes of the rich and famous' on her laptop and she breathed a sigh of relief.

Graham grabbed the car keys from the kitchen counter. 'Right, I'm off to run those errands. Just think, love – no more supermarket for us when we're loaded! We'll send our butler!' He whistled cheerily as he left the house.

Mum rubbed her temples. 'I've got a headache. Would you mind watching the kids this morning,

Pud? I just need a lie-down, but I'll be back down in time to take Tabby to her party,' she called over her shoulder. Of course, Pudding had nearly forgotten: Tabby had been invited to a friend's birthday party that afternoon.

Pudding helped Callum – who still seemed a bit grumpy and quiet – tidy up the breakfast things. Flying umbrellas, she was a bit pooped herself after a night of partying. She lay down on the sofa, resting her tired-from-dancing legs.

Hollywood! LA! The City of Angels . . . and now pandas. Back at the zoo, Pudding used to dream she was Mary Poppins, but she'd never thought it could really happen. It wasn't at all what she'd imagined when she'd arrived on the doorstep a year ago. Back then, all she'd wanted was to be a nanny, part of a real family like Mary Poppins was – but now she could have *both!* They would be going to America, together. A family adventure, for all of them. Her and Graham on the big screen, Cal and Tabby playing in the sunshine every day, swimming and rollerblading, and Pam . . . maybe she could take a well-earned break.

And she, Pudding Poppins, would be bringing home the bacon . . . and the sausages and the beans and the . . .

Pudding's eyes drifted shut and suddenly she was floating down from the sky, holding an umbrella, then, quick as a flash, she was in a lightsaber battle with Kylo Ren. Suddenly, she was atop the Empire State building, swatting planes,

a tiny Tabby in her paw, then running from a giant rolling stone with the Holy Grail in her furry grasp. She found Nemo, clicked her ruby-slippered heels together and drank a bamboo martini – shaken, not stirred.

Next, she was standing at the very front of the *Titanic*, her arms out wide, the chilly sea air rippling through her fur. 'I'm the queen of the world,' she shouted, as the huge ship suddenly crashed straight into a giant pudding.

Huh?

'Pudding!' Tabby was shaking her awake – she had fallen asleep on the sofa. 'Pudding, I need you – come on!'

Pudding shook the stars from her eyes and allowed a desperate-looking Tabby to hoist her to her feet.

She tugged at her paw, leading her towards the front door. 'Pudding, this is serious.'

'Tabby dear, goodness me, whatever is the matter?'

'You need to give me a Hollywood makeover – RIGHT NOW! Before the party!'

'Your party – of course! Let's make you look like the superstar you are,' Pudding said warmly.

Tabby bounded up the stairs towards the bathroom, Pudding hot on her heels.

Callum peered out of the kitchen as the two of them leapt upstairs. 'Pudding?'

'Yes, Callum?' Pudding said, hesitating halfway up.

While Pudding had been snoring, Callum had started investigating. But to his disappointment, he hadn't found anything suspicious on Penni P. Now his tummy was starting to rumble. 'You will make us lunch, right?'

'Oh, Callum, there's plenty of snacks in the kitchen. You'll live,' Pudding sang. She followed Tabby, taking the stairs two at a time, the house shaking.

Cal rummaged in the cupboards for something that resembled a healthy, nutritious lunch, trying to ignore the shrieks and giggles from upstairs. Mum must be exhausted if she was sleeping through that racket.

He sat on the floor and tore open a box of Wheatihoops. How was he going to get the evidence he needed to convince the family that Penni was trouble?

He drummed his fingers on the cereal box, eventually spotting the super free gift offer on the back: a secret spy kit!

That's it! he thought. *I need to spy on her. She's bound to slip up sooner or later.*

'But I can't do it on my own,' he muttered to himself.

He needed a team, like the Avengers – or at the very least, a sidekick – right now! He didn't have any time to lose. But who would help him?

If only Neil were here, he'd understand. Cal sighed. Neil knew all about Pudding. After all, he was Cal's best friend in the world. But he wouldn't be able to visit until the school holidays, now his family had moved away.

Dad would be hopeless. But what about Mum? She was the most down-to-earth of all of them, and she was an adult too, which would certainly be useful. But would she consent to him spying on Penni P, let alone helping him? He didn't think so. Besides, she had to take Tabby to a party.

That struck Tabby off the list too – though as a seven-year-old girl with a pretty loud mouth, she probably wouldn't have been a great spy anyway.

That only left one person. Pudding herself.

Cal groaned.

CHAPTER 5
Spy Panda

Once Tabby and Mum had left, Pudding clapped her paws together. 'Just you and me, Cal! Do you want to help me run through my lines?' Pudding brandished a sheaf of paper she'd printed from the internet. 'It's the actual script! I may as well get ahead of the game!'

But Callum pulled the script out of Pudding's paw and shook his head.

'I've got something else in mind. You won't like

it,' he said, 'but hear me out.'

Twenty minutes later, Pudding was dressed in a voluminous black raincoat from Dad's costume collection with the hood pulled up over her face and a pair of large sunglasses over her eyes. 'I'm still not sure about this, Callum,' she said. 'Penni P is a good person, and she's giving us the biggest opportunity of our lives.'

'Then there'll be nothing to see, will there?' Callum said firmly, pulling his own nondescript black hoody over his head. 'Here's the address of the paper she works at.' He brandished a Post-it. 'I thought we could start there, wait for her to go out, then follow her. It's not far from here – we can go on our scooters.' He paused, then added, 'Thanks for doing this, Pudding. It means a lot, even if you think I'm wrong.'

'Well, you *did* promise me we'd do a full rehearsal later,' Pudding said, '*complete with dances*!'

Callum grimaced but nodded.

'Then let's go!'

Callum and Pudding headed off on their scooters down the street towards the edge of town, towards the offices of the *Edinburgh Tattle*. Pudding had to perch on Callum's scooter, the bigger of the two, which meant Callum was stuck with Tabby's, which had pink sparkly streamers on the handles. Not exactly spy-like, but it couldn't be helped.

Time to put 'Operation Spend a Penni' into action.

When they reached the office, they threw their scooters in a nearby bush and crept towards the front door.

'You wait out here,' Cal said to Pudding. 'I'll go in and see if she's here.' He wiped his sweaty hands on his jogging bottoms as a serious-looking man in a suit left the building, then he tiptoed inside. He suddenly felt as though he were about to give a performance at the theatre, like Dad – and he was pretty sure he had stage fright. Dad had said something to him years ago about that and Cal hadn't been sure what he'd meant.

Now he understood.

His mouth was dry and his hands shook, as he tried to think about what he was going to say. What if he went to speak and no words came out? This acting business was much harder than it looked.

He cleared his throat as he approached the reception desk. 'Penni P?' he croaked.

Behind the desk was a young-looking man – much older than Cal, of course, but not as old as Mum and Dad. He put down his phone. 'Pardon?' he said.

Cal placed his palms on the reception desk to

steady himself. 'Is Penni P here?' he managed, through gritted teeth.

The receptionist looked amused. 'Penny . . . pea?' Then his expression changed. 'Ohhh, Penny P! Right.' Then he sniggered. 'Well, I wouldn't know, sorry.'

Cal frowned. 'But she does work here?'

The man was still grinning. 'Och, sure. She works here. Penn-eee.' He put a weird emphasis on the eee and laughed.

Cal shuffled from one foot to the other. 'Could you give her this, please. Thank you. Um, goodbye.' He slid an envelope across the desk, then backed out of the office building, almost bouncing off Pudding who had been waiting with her nose pressed to the glass door.

They ran to the verge where their scooters were stashed and Cal fell to the grass, panting. He was not cut out for espionage . . . or acting.

'What was that? What did you give him?' Pudding asked, when they had got their breath back.

'A letter for Penni P,' Callum said, blushing furiously.

'Oh, Callum,' Pudding sighed. 'You didn't say anything about us, did you? If you mess up my big chance I'm going to be really cross.'

'Let's just—' Callum said, focusing on the glass doors again. 'Look!' Through the leaves he saw a familiar face leaving the *Tattle* building, with a letter in her hand. *His* letter. 'There she is!' Rummaging in the bag again, he pulled out a pair of binoculars and a pirate telescope, which he handed to Pudding.

'What did you say in that—' Pudding whispered, but Cal cut her off.

'Ssh!' Cal made himself as small as he could behind the bush.

Penni P was now reading his note. Pudding huffed a bit too loudly for Cal's liking, rustling the foliage they were hiding in. Penni P looked across at the bush and stood up, heading in their direction.

Callum's tummy twisted and sweat prickled down the back of his neck. He was sure they'd been spotted, and Penni's face was full of frosty fury . . . but then, a few paces away from the bush, she stopped at a

rubbish bin and threw the note inside.

Close call, thought Callum, allowing himself to breathe again.

Penni P was still barely a few paces away from

Callum and Pudding's hiding place when her phone rang.

Cal held his breath again from behind a faceful of greenery and listened closely.

'Ugh, you read my mind,' moaned Penni. 'It's like you always know when I need to talk. Can you meet me for a coffee? I really need to talk to you . . . and I need a favour.' She paused.

Pudding had started birdwatching with her telescope and Cal nudged her to make sure she was listening.

'I am having the worst day. First of all, that man! I swear I'm going to nominate him for Most Awful Boss of the Year. How can he not see my potential? I'm the most talented journalist in this dump, by a mile. Well, they'll see. I'm going to slay them with this panda thing and then he'll be sorry. I'll have the story of the year – it's HUGE! – and I'll be taking it with me when I get the call from *The Times*. And in case there was any doubt, someone has just sent me a note which confirms all my expectations.'

Cal felt sick as he realized his plan had backfired – the threatening note to 'stay away from Pudding' (he'd spent ages cutting letters out of newspapers to spell it out!) had simply confirmed to Penni that she was on to something.

Penni looked livid. But, soothed by the voice on the other end of the line, she eventually sighed. 'You're right, of course. I'll just keep working on it and . . . sorry, what?' She took a long-overdue breath. 'Yes, I can get some loo roll on my way home. OK. See you in a few minutes.'

Cal grabbed Pudding by the sleeve of her huge raincoat. 'Did you hear that? She knows! She knows you're real – you have to believe me now!'

Pudding put down her telescope. 'That's not

what I heard,' she said, patting Callum on the head kindly. 'You're in a flap about nothing, Callum. The poor woman is simply unhappy in her job. Her boss sounds like a nightmare.'

Cal stared at her, eyes practically on stalks. 'You weren't listening?'

'Of course I was listening! Penni P thinks our success story is going to knock her boss's socks off.' There were stars in Pudding's eyes. 'She's discovered us and she thinks we're going to be HUGE!' She gazed down at Callum. 'Let's go home now, there's still time to read through—'

'No, not yet,' Callum said, feeling desperate. 'We're not done yet. *Please*, Pudding. Let's follow her to her coffee meeting. Please?'

Pudding hesitated, then sighed. 'All right, but this is it. No more snooping around. After this, we go home and you help me practise my lines.'

'Yes!' Callum jumped on to Tabby's pink sparkly scooter.

Pudding grabbed her own scooter, flipped her dark glasses back down and tucked her ears neatly inside her hood. 'Come on then, let's go.'

CHAPTER 6
Panda-nappers?

Cal and Pudding scooted after Penni as she hurried towards the local shops. Sticking to the pavement, they whizzed past parked cars and zoomed round benches, crouching down on their scooters to be less conspicuous – though it is difficult not to attract attention when one of you is a panda in a raincoat.

Tabby's scooter was a nightmare though, and it squeaked and rattled so much that Cal was certain it would blow their cover. Then Callum got tangled up in a dog lead, a confused-looking dachshund on one end and a cross owner on the other.

After that, they ditched their rides behind a large wheelie bin and carried on, on foot, ducking into doorways and behind benches and lamp posts, straining to keep Penni P in sight. Then, Pudding lost her sunglasses doing a fancy combat roll and they had to go back for them, almost losing their target.

Penni had walked quite far ahead, weaving in and out of shoppers and tourists, and they dashed to catch up, pushing through a queue of people at a cash machine.

Suddenly, from behind, a bus honked its horn and Penni looked round almost directly at them. Cal and Pudding pinned themselves to the wall of the bank like cartoon characters.

'That was close,' said Pudding. 'Cal, I really think

you should've put more effort into your undercover costume. You stick out a mile.'

Cal stared at his panda friend, speechless. Then he caught sight of Penni slipping into a familiar chain cafe. 'Look, she's gone inside.'

'Marvellous! I could do with a muffin – this undercover detective work is very draining.'

Inside, Penni P took a seat in a booth, opposite a dark-haired woman. Pudding hurried into the booth next door while Callum ordered the drinks – a double frappuccino mocha choca latte with bamboo milk for Pudding, of course, and a hot chocolate for Cal.

By the time Callum sat down with the drinks, and a pile of free reading material as a decoy, the two women were talking about . . . nail salons.

'Anything interesting so far?' Callum whispered.

Pudding yawned. 'No. And there won't be anything, Callum. You'll see.' She rustled a copy of the *Hollywood Times.*

Then Penni and her friend moved on to the best time to plant spring bulbs.

Callum sipped his hot chocolate and drew faces on the people in *Ideal Homes* magazine. Pudding pored

over the 'red carpet style' pages.

Next Penni started to explain an entire plot-line of a popular soap.

Pudding slid off her stool. 'Nature calls – and we ought to be getting home when I'm back. Sorry, Callum, but there's really nothing for us to hear.' She set off for the cafe loos.

Cal's tummy grumbled and he gazed at the muffins at the counter. Maybe Pudding was right. Maybe he'd been mistaken. Maybe this was all some big—

'So, why are we really here, Pen?'

Callum's ears perked up.

'Oh, Amber – I'm on to something. I'm going to need your help, but first hear me out.' She took a sip of her tea and began. 'You remember the panda that escaped from the zoo last year?'

Amber nodded. Callum's stomach twisted. He stared at the loo door, unable to believe this was happening when Pudding wasn't at the table.

'I knew something dodgy was going on when I first covered that story – zoo enclosures left open, that doddery old fool, Gerald the zookeeper, and then all of a sudden the panda's found in China? Suspicious. So anyway, a week ago I get a call from this guy – well, *boy* really – who says he's got information about the panda. He tells me he wants to remain anonymous, but I heard his dad, or someone, yelling at him in the background. He shouted,' Penni put on a gruff voice. '"MIKE SPIKER, GET OOT MA KITCHEN YA SCABBY WEE . . ." It was quite funny really.'

Cal almost chuckled at Penni's impression of Spud Spiker, but then he realized what she was saying. Mike Spiker had tipped off Penni about Pudding! His blood went almost as hot as his hot chocolate.

Penni continued. 'He told me that he was living opposite a family who had a real, live panda – and that they were using it in the hit show *Panda-mime*. Well, of course I assumed it was a prank call – probably someone at the *Tattle*, jealous of my talents – but I decided to go along to the show anyway. I knew they weren't doing interviews which is a bit suspicious in itself, isn't it? But I managed to get one anyway, thanks to my super-duper journalist skills. And Amber, here's the thing: Pudding is not someone in a costume – she's an animal, cruelly kept in a house and made to perform!'

Amber and Callum gasped at the same time. *Oh no*, thought Callum, *she's half right – but she's really got the wrong end of the stick!* He looked desperately towards the loos.

'What about the note you mentioned?' asked Amber. 'You said it confirmed everything?'

'It was from one of them. The Campbells. Threatening me to keep away. But not Penni P – I will not be frightened off.'

Cal put his head in his hands. The note wasn't meant to be a threat. It was a plea, as in: please, leave my panda alone. The marshmallows in his tummy started feeling sticky and unwelcome. How had this got so out of hand? All he wanted was for his family to be happy.

'Oh my goodness – that poor panda, being panda-napped!' said Amber. 'Of course I'll help, lovely, but only as long as it's not going to get you in trouble. I'm worried about you. These panda-nappers could be dangerous.'

'It's fine – trust me. If I can pull this off, it'll be the scoop of the century . . . Well, for the *Tattle* anyway . . . And obviously I want to do what's right for the panda.' She said this like it was a bit of an afterthought.

'So, why do you need my help?' Amber asked.

'Well, you're an actor, so . . .' She paused. 'I need you to pretend to be a top Hollywood producer.'

'What?' Cal could tell that Amber had almost spat out her coffee. 'That doesn't sound very ethical, Penni.'

'Just hear me out. Your name will be Amber di Angelo. We can go over the details later, but basically

I need you to charm these Campbells with talk of *Lights, Camera, Action,* and try and get them to open up about where the panda has come from. Maybe we could even get a confession! I'll record everything. While you're doing that, I'll try and figure out which one of them is on to me and get absolute proof of pandahood. How does that sound?'

Cal almost cried out, but somehow managed to keep his cool. At least now he knew Penni's next move: a pretend 'audition' with Amber. Somehow he would have to stop this 'meeting' — their family life depended on it.

CHAPTER 7
Hollywood Fever

As they hopped off their scooters outside the house, Callum tried to convince Pudding for the millionth time that he was telling the truth. 'I'm serious – that Mike Spiker put her up to it.' He glanced over at the Spikers' house, feeling that hot-chocolate heat run through his blood again. 'There's no movie, no Hollywood deal, it's all a trick to get her face on the front page of her stupid newspaper.' Cal wiped his eyes on his sleeve, but Pudding wasn't impressed.

'Callum, I understand you're afraid of change, but it's a little convenient that you heard all this while I was in the toilet and not around to hear it.'

Callum wheeled the scooters round the back of the house. 'Actually, it's very INconvenient.' He kicked his scooter as he leant it up against the wall. Pudding's weight had bowed it a little in the middle.

'Mary Poppins taught me that it's a good thing to be very kind but very firm,' Pudding said, drawing herself up and placing Mum's flowerpot on her head. 'So now, Callum, as your panda nanny, it's time for me to put a stop to this nonsense.'

'Pudding, please, you have to—'

'I've been nice about the whole thing, but this is where it ends, all right?' She looked at him with her best attempt at sternness, though being as fluffy as she was didn't help.

Callum didn't see anything for it but to lie through his teeth. 'All right,' he said.

Back inside, he tiptoed along the hall and into the kitchen, expecting to be led by the smell of cooking, but there was none. Pudding went upstairs to 'powder her nose' while Callum found Mum, Dad and Tabby watching something with bright lights, beaches and palm trees on the telly. Well, Tabby was zonked out on the armchair, an empty party bag on her lap and cake crumbs scattered all over her party dress. Classic post-sugar coma.

'Mum?' Cal said nervously.

Mum paused the TV and looked up from the writing pad on her lap. Had she been taking notes? 'Cal, hen, hello. You've been quiet,' she said.

Er, I've been gone. And so has Pudding! They *hadn't even noticed* . . . sure, that was what he'd wanted, but actually it felt weird and horrible. They hadn't even realized that he and Pudding were missing! Anything could've happened to them.

'What's for tea?'

Graham looked at his watch. 'Och, would ye look at the time! I suppose we'd better get a takeaway. Cal, be a good lad and grab the menu.'

Mum pressed play on the TV remote and turned back to the screen.

Callum sighed.

Over the next few days, things got even worse.

Penni P had called about setting up a video call with 'Amber, my hotshot producer friend in Los Angeles'. As a result, what Callum called 'Hollywood Fever' had tightened its grip on the family. Pudding spent all her time running through the *Mary Poppins* script and dressing up in glamorous outfits with Tabby – she never seemed to have time to help Cal with his homework any more, and they hadn't had any panda cakes since the interview at the theatre. Mum spent all her time researching schools in LA, while Dad had turned into a total diva.

Hollywood was all anyone talked about.

Cal had no hope of stopping them going to the so-called meeting with Amber. They just weren't interested in anything else. He even tried telling them what he'd been up to at school, which he never normally did, but even that couldn't break through the movie-mania.

It was like if you weren't Penni P's number one fan, you might as well not exist.

Cal sat on his bed, staring out of the window. Everything seemed so hopeless. Why was Penni Rotten Mouldy Pea trying to hurt them? What had they ever done to her? She claimed to be looking out for Pudding, but that was rubbish. All she cared about was the story – a big, headline-hitting scoop: she'd found a real live panda pretending to be a fake panda, who was on stage pretending to be a real panda.

Tears ran down Callum's face.

He was glad he wasn't interested in fame. It seemed to make people do weird things. Even Pudding, who was the kindest person he knew, had got carried along by the wave of everyone's excitement. She really thought she was going to be Mary Poppins, the practically perfect nanny. But she'd forgotten she already *was* a nanny – his nanny. It was like she'd forgotten what that meant.

Well, he hadn't forgotten – Pudding was *his* panda and he wasn't going to let some mushy Pea woman take her away.

Cal knew he had to do something, but what could he, a ten-year-old invisible boy, do? What he needed was some proper outside help. Someone who wasn't caught up in all of this. If only Neil hadn't moved.

Just because he's moved doesn't mean I can't talk to him, Callum realized.

He went down to the landline phone in the hall and tapped in his best mate's number. Luckily, he was in.

'What's up, Callum? How is everyone?'

Callum took a shuddering breath.

'Hey, what's wrong?'

'Listen, I need your advice.' And Callum told him everything – from the ill-fated interview to tailing Penni P in the cafe. 'The trouble is,' he finished, 'no one believes me and I don't know who else to turn to.'

'Hmm,' Neil said. 'Well, it

has to be someone who already knows and cares about Pudding, doesn't it? That must narrow down the field a lot. Did she have any friends before she came to you?'

'No, I don't—' Cal broke off, remembering the photo Pudding had stuck to her dressing-room mirror. *Gerald!* A grin spread over his face. 'Neil, you're a genius!'

'Anytime, pal,' Neil said, sounding a little smug.

Once they'd hung up, Callum ran through the reasoning again. Gerald had been Pudding's old keeper at the zoo. He definitely cared about Pudding and he wouldn't want anything bad to happen to her. Plus, Cal had Gerald's work email address from when he had adopted Pudding in the first place.

He might just be able to help.

He headed upstairs and began to type out an email on his tablet.

CHAPTER 8
Cruella de P

The next day, the Campbells were gathered round a rather flash laptop on a marble table, in the lounge area of a very posh hotel. The room was quiet, apart from the delicate tapping of china teacups and silver spoons.

They were all squeezed on to a green velvety sofa. Mum looked anxious, alternating between checking her hair and shrinking in her seat, away from the attention. Dad and Pudding were quietly running through the words to 'Supercalifragilisticexpialidocious' – their musical number, in case Amber wanted them to audition – and Tabby was on Pudding's lap, sipping water from a tiny glass, her little finger pointing out like she was taking high tea at the palace. Beside them sat Penni P, back in her fancy clothes and hairdo, waiting for 'my very important friend, Amber di Angelo' to send the video link.

Callum was perched on a tiny wooden stool, like a guest at a birthday party who wasn't actually invited. Not that he wanted to be there – he didn't want any of them to be there, but of course no one had listened to him.

Cal had moved on from being upset to furious with both Penni and Mike Spiker – but also with himself.

'OK, we're ready,' announced Penni P. 'I'll just click here to join and we'll be "live to LA".'

Dad leant across the table. 'Callum, if you don't want to be involved, that's fine,' he said, too quietly for Amber to hear. 'Obviously we all wish you would, but if you can't say anything nice, then don't say anything at all. And keep that face out of view. You look like we're making you live with the Spikers.'

I'd rather be living with the Spikers than sitting here, Cal thought angrily. But of course he didn't say it.

Penni suddenly looked at him, as if she were only just noticing he was there. 'Have we met?'

Cal shook his head and scowled.

'Callum Campbell, that's not very polite,' scolded Mum. 'I apologize, Miss P. He's had a very hard week at school.'

As if you'd know, Cal thought.

'Ooh, here she is!' Penni pointed her now perfectly manicured fingernails at the screen. Right on cue, Mum popped a big toffee in Tabby's mouth to keep her quiet – *that'll keep her chewing for a while*, Callum thought glumly. 'Amber dahhhling, how are you? Can you hear me OK from *all the way across the world* ?'

On screen was the dark-haired woman Callum had seen in the cafe. She was sitting outside in the sunshine, under a parasol, a high hedge behind her and palm trees creeping into view on her left.

It didn't look like Scotland. But then, neither had their video of Pudding 'back in China'!

'Hey there, Penni, and hey, Campbells. How are y'all doing?' Her accent sounded American too.

Just as they were getting started, a young girl came over to ask Pudding for an autograph. It was such perfect timing, Cal wondered if Penni had paid her to do it. Or perhaps he was being paranoid. Had he got it wrong? Could he have?

Amber seemed delighted. 'Oh, Puddin', you are such a superstar already. You're gonna be just perfect for this role. Now I know you are a mime act right now, but Penni tells me that, whoever you are inside that costume, you are actually a terrific actress with a great singing voice too. So tell me a little about yourself . . . I don't suppose you're going to tell me who's in the suit, are you?' She laughed, then looked serious. 'Unless it's not a suit at all.' There was an agonizing silence and Cal saw Penni's eyes go as wide as an American dinner plate, then Amber laughed. 'But seriously, it's such a great outfit. Who made it?'

As Amber carried on, playing her role to perfection, telling them how wonderful they were and how exciting it was all going to be, Callum kept his eyes fixed on Penni.

Penni, in turn, was studying Pudding.

Every now and then, she put her arm around Pud, like when Amber gave her a compliment, or asked Penni's opinion on Pudding's acting. It was subtle, but each time it happened, Penni gave Pud a little stroke or fiddled with her fur.

She was also taking a lot of photos of Pudding on her phone. Amber carried on her questioning. It was obvious Penni had told her to keep asking where Pudding had come from, and how they had all met. It was really forcing Mum and Dad to concentrate, and Cal could see Penni watching Dad closely to see if she could spot his lips moving. After all, *she* believed that Pudding was a real panda. And apart from Doctor Dolittle, whoever had ever heard of a talking panda? Tabby was still furiously chewing her toffee.

Cal wiggled his stool closer to Penni, and just as she was about to touch Pudding again, he elbowed her.

Don't touch my panda, he thought.

'Sorry. The stool's a bit wobbly,' he said, and looked at her in a way he hoped was mean and tough.

Penni looked at him in surprise, then her expression turned to sudden recognition. 'You followed me in the cafe,' she whispered, as Pudding and Dad did one of their jokes for Amber. 'I saw you leaving!' Cal could almost feel her making the connections in her brain. She looked at Amber and back to him. 'Oh!' She leapt up, knocking the laptop backwards, but before she could say anything else, a waiter came over to take their drinks orders.

As the others ordered coffees and milkshakes, and one towering afternoon tea, Callum glared at her. 'That's right – I saw you and Amber in the coffee shop and I heard what you said. I know what you're up to.'

She glowered at him. 'And I know what *you're* up to. You won't get away with it.'

'Us? We just want to be left alone. Pudding is part of our family,' he hissed. 'We're not getting away with anything. Why don't you just go away?' It came out louder than he anticipated, and everyone turned to look, including a family checking in at the reception desk over the other side of the room.

'CALLUM!' Dad took a sharp, deep breath.

Amber's voice came from the screen. 'Hey there, Campbells, we lost a bit of connection there. Is everything OK with y'all?'

Dad composed himself. 'Oh yes, absolutely Ms di

Angelo. All just perfect.'

Penni was still standing. 'While you show Amber what you can do, why don't I take Cal to look at the portraits?' she suggested, grabbing him by the wrist before he could protest. 'Lots of famous people come here and their pictures are on the wall.' She hauled him to his feet, her nails digging into his skin. 'I bet Pudding's portrait will be up there before long. The public need to see her.' Penni smiled for the others' benefit. 'Who she *really* is,' she added, just for Cal to hear.

'You just want to tear my family apart,' Callum said, feeling close to tears as they walked a few paces away from the table.

'I'm trying to help the bear,' she lied through gritted teeth. 'I want justice for her. She deserves to be free!'

'Rubbish, you just want to get on the front page

of your crummy newspaper.'

Callum yanked his arm out of Penni's grip, not realizing the waiter had come back and was standing right behind them with their drinks. His hand smacked the tray, flipping it into the air, drinks and all.

A whole banana smoothie with extra sprinkles, ice cream and strawberries on top drenched Pudding from head to hind paw.

She squealed and leapt up, spraying everyone with yellow milk.

Tabby wailed. The banana smoothie had, of course, been her drink.

Penni, who was now wearing an iced latte, scooped a blob of strawberry ice cream and sprinkles from Pudding's lap and threw it back at Callum.

Callum leapt out of the way, and the gooey mess hit the hotel manager square in the face as he stormed in to see what the fuss was all about.

'Who did that?' he roared.

Cal and Penni pointed at each other.

'You'll pay for this!' he said, his voice shaking as he wiped sprinkles from his perfectly curled moustache. 'This is a respectable hotel. Never in all my days—' He stamped his foot to make the point, but slipped on a strawberry, falling backwards into a leather armchair, his legs in the air.

Callum couldn't help himself and laughed out loud.

Dad was almost as red in the face as the manager. 'That's it, I'm taking you home, young man.'

Tabby yelled, 'No! We can't go yet – I haven't had my milkshake!'

Mum had slid so far out of sight she was almost under the table, but Cal could still see her look of sad disappointment. 'Yes, I think we ought to leave,' she said to Amber apologetically.

'I think that's a good idea,' said Penni. She looked directly at Callum. 'I have everything I need . . . I mean, I'm sure Amber has everything *she* needs.' She opened her palm to show Cal what was in her grasp: a tuft of unmistakably *real* black-and-white fur. Smiling like Cruella de Vil gazing on her spotted puppies, she murmured, 'I'll be in touch.'

CHAPTER 9
Penelope Busybody

Callum found himself indefinitely grounded for what Dad had called his 'selfish' behaviour. Cal hadn't bothered trying to argue, even though his behaviour had been the absolute opposite of selfish. He was trying to save his entire family, but for some reason no one seemed to care.

He didn't mind too much about being grounded, though. It gave him time to think about what to do next. Perhaps he could make them see that they couldn't afford the plane tickets. Or remind Mum that Tabby got travel sick? Or point out to Dad that he hated the heat?

But it was no good. They were too far gone to listen to sense – it didn't even seem to matter that Pud didn't have a passport. To every objection Cal raised, they always had the same answer: 'Penni P is sorting it out.'

Cal slumped on his bed and sighed. He stared at the posters on his wall – his favourite Avengers, a comic-strip drawing of King Arthur and the poster for *Panda-mime*. He loved the show; he was so happy for Pudding and Dad that they had found something they both loved. And they made so many people happy.

Just not him.

Pudding was supposed to be his. She should be there for him. After all, that's what she first came for – to be a nanny for an unhappy boy.

But he couldn't remember the last time Pudding had really been there for him. Not when he needed help with a puzzle, or a cuddle after Mike Spiker had been mean to him. What was the point of having a panda for a special friend, if you still felt this unhappy?

That afternoon, Dad and Pudding had left for the Saturday matinee of *Panda-mime,* and Tabby had her head buried in the latest sparkly *Warrior Unicorns* book. To Cal, it felt like the first time in weeks the house was quiet.

'I know we've not been paying much attention to you, Callum,' said Mum, as they finished preparing sandwiches together. 'But really, what is the matter? That outburst earlier was so unlike you.'

'I know, I'm sorry. I didn't mean to cause such a fuss. I just got so angry because . . .' His words tailed off. What was the point? No one believed him.

Then again, this was Mum. Callum decided to give it one more try.

'Do you want to go to Hollywood, Mum?'

'Of course. I mean, it'll be very different and, well, it wouldn't be my first choice, but . . . how can we not give Dad and Pudding the chance to live their dreams? This is a once in a lifetime opportunity for them.'

Cal nodded. 'It is, isn't it? So don't you think it's even a little bit strange? Penni P, who we have never heard of, suddenly turns up wanting an interview that we promised we'd never give, and just happens to have a movie friend who's remaking *Mary Poppins* . . . who just happens to be Pudding's idol. Isn't it a bit of a coincidence?'

Mum sighed as they sat down on the sofa with their lunch. 'Not this again, Cal.'

'But Mum, please. Penni P is lying! I heard her with my own ears. It was Mike Spiker who tipped her off about Pudding.' He slammed his hand on the cushion, making his cheese sandwich jump off the plate. 'This whole thing is just him getting revenge!'

Mum dusted crumbs off the seat. 'Och, Cal. You and your dad do love a wee bit o' drama. But it's so nice to see Dad happy and successful. Let's not put a downer on that. You should be happy too.'

'But isn't it worse to get Dad's hopes up? Because if we don't stop her, Penni P is going to have Pudding taken away and Dad exposed as some kind of animal-exploiting baddie . . .' Cal blinked back angry tears. 'Everything will go back to how it was before. *He'll* be like he was before. I can't go back to that – it was horrible.'

He thought back to how upset Dad had been last year. Enough that he had walked out one morning and gone missing, even if he had only gone as far as the shed. And that had just been because of money trouble. Now that Pudding was part of their family, losing her would be so much worse.

Mum folded her arms. 'What do you mean, she wants to take Pudding away?'

'Mum. I've told you this already. She knows that *Panda-mime* doesn't star a person in a panda suit, but a *real* panda! She's going to name and shame us on the front page of the newspaper and the zoo people will come and take Pud away and we'll all go to jail for panda-napping and bear-fraud . . .' Callum made a snort-sobbing sound and took a bite of his lunch to cover it up. He almost choked.

Mum leant back on the sofa. 'I see.'

Once he'd safely swallowed, Cal looked at her anxiously over his sandwich. Had she listened?

'When you put it like that, it *is* all a bit sudden.' She grabbed Cal's hand. 'Promise me you are telling the truth about Penni?'

Cal's heart was racing, but he tried his best to look serious and grown-up and very, very honest. 'Cross my heart,' he said solemnly.

Mum bit her bottom lip. 'I've always worried this might happen. I've never said it out loud, but having a talking panda in the family is a heavy secret to carry. There was always the chance someone could find out.'

Cal had never thought of secrets as being heavy before, but Mum was right: it was weighing him down. 'So what do we do?'

'The problem with secrets is, the longer you carry them, the heavier they get. The only way to lighten your load is to let them go.' Mum was looking at him with her kindly face, but that didn't make what she

was saying any easier to understand.

'What I mean, Cal, is that sometimes honesty is the best policy. We might just have to tell the whole truth.'

Callum leapt off the sofa. 'What? We can't! They'll definitely take her away. Everyone will find out that she didn't go back to China and we kept her, and that we're the ones lying and Dad's show will be over and, and—' Cal burst into tears. 'Please don't tell, Mum. Please don't let them take Pudding away.'

Mum pulled Cal into a bear hug of her own. 'Don't you worry, Callum. No one is taking our Pudding. We'll figure something out.'

'Mum,' Callum said, 'I actually already had an idea – well, Neil did really.' He told her about the call with his best friend and how he'd sent a message to Pudding's old keeper, Gerald.

'I don't like the idea of you getting in touch with

strangers, poppet,' Mum said, a little sternly, though she softened it with a smile. 'But ... talking to Gerald doesn't sound like a bad plan. We certainly need all the help we can get. Let's wait and see if he replies.'

They didn't have to wait long. Cal was delighted when, the next day, he answered the door to a man with a bushy moustache in a flat cap. It had to be Gerald!

'Ah, you must be Callum? Poor wee lad – I got your email. How's things wi' ye?'

That was the nicest thing anyone had said to him in ages.

As Cal showed him to the living room, they talked about school, and then Gerald told Callum he had just retired – one of his ex-colleagues had forwarded on Cal's email. Cal didn't mind the sound of retirement at all – no school, no work. What could be better? But

Gerald confessed he was a bit bored, and he missed all his animals.

'So . . . what did you think of my email?' asked Cal as they sat down.

'I didnae understand much o' it. You lads and lassies really need to learn to write in complete sentences,' said Gerald, smiling. 'But I was so happy to hear that ma wee Pudding was happy and living with a family too – it fair made this auld man's heart sing, ma laddie – but I could tell ye were also upset and feelin' alone. What's all this about, then?'

Mum came in with tea and Bourbon biscuits. 'Perfect timing, Gerald. It's lovely to meet you. Any friend of Pudding's is a friend of ours.'

'As you can see, I'm not so alone any more,' Cal said, smiling up at his mum gratefully. 'I've got one family member onside. We just need your help with the rest.'

'Well, if it helps you and ma wee Pudding out, I'm your man. Especially if you keep these biccies coming.'

Callum filled Gerald in about Penni P and the

promise of Hollywood, the virtual meeting with Amber di Angelo, or whatever her real name was, and what he had overheard in the cafe previously.

Gerald listened carefully and when Cal had finished he stroked his moustache and nodded. 'Penni P, you say. And she works at the *Tattle*?'

Gerald got out his phone. 'Give me a minute. I'm not as quick with these infernal things as you youngsters.' A few moments later, he held it out so Cal and his mum could see. 'This her?'

Cal frowned. 'Yes! Though she looks different now.' The Penni in the picture was wearing train-track braces and glasses. Her hair was frizzy and brown

and she looked a lot younger.

'Looks like she's had a big makeover,' Mum said. 'How do you know her, Gerald?'

'Well, that explains a lot,' said Gerald, roughly. 'This, ma lovely Campbells, is Penelope Peabody, Junior Writer at the *Tattle*. Penelope Busybody, I call her. Ugh, she's always been a pest that one, ever since she started a couple of years ago. They put her on the Entertainment section, so she was always popping up at the zoo, poking her nose around – determined to find some scandal for the front page. That lady disnae understand that news can be positive too – she thinks she needs some big bad news to make her career, and it sounds like she's decided that's you.'

Cal leant back and took in what Gerald was saying. Penni P wasn't the super-journalist she claimed to be. She was a junior writer, and not a particularly good one, if Gerald was to be believed.

'Before we left the hotel, Penni took some of Pudding's fur,' said Cal. 'I think she's going to use it to prove that Pudding is real. We have to stop her. You know Penni P best, Gerald. What do we do?'

'Well, I'll tell you – people like Penelope, you have to play them at their own game,' Gerald said, smiling. 'But first, you have to get Pudding and Graham onside.'

CHAPTER 10

The Truth in Black and White

From his room, Cal heard Mum welcoming Penni into their home and Dad being over-the-top friendly as usual.

Cal's stomach went all knotty for about the fiftieth time since Gerald had left with a wink and a 'good luck, laddie'.

Poor Dad, poor Pudding, to have had their dreams shattered like that.

Mum had broken the news to them, since she was

the only one they would have believed. Even then, they hadn't – at first. But once they did, they'd been so brave. Despite Cal being annoyed at not being listened to, he was very proud of how they'd taken the news – so proud he hadn't even said 'I told you so' a single time.

Now Callum turned to face the portrait on his wall of his hero, King Arthur. 'If there's any way you could see fit to give me a hand with this, I'd appreciate it. If we fail, Pudding will probably be put back in a zoo. We'll never see her again, and I guess we'll all go to prison.' He touched Excalibur. 'Well, wish me luck.'

Then he took a deep breath and went downstairs.

'How come we're allowed chocolate ones all of a sudden?' asked Tabby, reaching for her second biscuit.

'Tabs. They're for our special guest,' said Mum,

smiling at Penni. 'Thanks so much for coming over. We're all so sorry the meeting with Amber ended the way it did. Callum, aren't you sorry?'

They'd talked about this. The apology was part of putting Penni at ease – before they sprang the trap. 'I'm really sorry,' he said.

'That's quite all right.' Penni was obviously feeling sure of herself. So sure, she couldn't stop smiling. In fact, she looked positively triumphant. 'Now

you're all gathered, I suppose this is as good a time as any to bring you my news.'

Pudding clapped her paws together.

'Oh, how exciting!' said Graham, hugging Pudding with one arm and Mum with the other. 'Is it about the movie? Did Amber like us?'

Penni gulped, and for a moment she seemed lost for words. *She feels bad*, Callum realized. And all of a sudden he felt a surge of hope.

'Well, I mean. I have news. Yes, I said that, didn't I?' She took a mouthful of tea and Cal could see her hands were shaking. She pulled herself together. 'It's no good, Campbells. I'm sorry, but I am a reporter and I have a duty to my readers, and to the world to uncover the truth. You might *seem* like nice people, but I know that you're not.'

'The truth?' Graham said.

'What is it exactly that you think you've found

out?' asked Mum.

Penni took a deep breath and squared her shoulders. 'Well, Pamela, it all began when I received a strange phone call from one of your neighbours. They alerted me to a major irregularity in your so-called "phenomenal stage show" and I went along to see for myself.

'I could hardly believe my eyes – not just that you, Graham Campbell, had the audacity to parade a real live panda around on stage, but that no one else in the audience seemed to have any clue! I've never seen such arrogance and ignorance in one place.'

Cal could see how much this hurt Graham and Pudding, but they did their best to hide it.

'But how did you get a real live panda? That was the question,' Penni continued. 'I knew I had to get a closer look, so I asked for an interview, and what should I find in your dressing room, Pudding, but a photo of an old adversary of mine on your mirror. Geriatric Gerald! I've had to do a number of exposés on goings-on at Edinburgh Zoo, I can tell you. But it got me thinking – what was the photo doing there? Gerald was a zookeeper. And not just any zookeeper, but the former guardian of a certain escaped panda. An escaped panda who, I later found out, was called Pudding.' Penni stared at the bear in question accusingly.

Now! thought Callum.

'Of course I'm a panda,' said Pudding, clear as a bell, meeting Penni's gaze.

Penni gasped, dropped the laptop she was holding and knocked over her plate of chocolate-chip cookies.

'What gave it away?' Pudding continued. 'The big paws? The black-and-white fur? It wouldn't be *Panda-mime* without a panda.'

'Y-y-you're not only real but you can—' Penni

stuttered.

'I'm not sure what your point is, Penni. So what? Here I am.'

Then Penni appeared to come to her senses. She turned to Dad. 'Very good. You can throw your voice. You can stop now, Graham – I get it: your ventriloquism skills are not in question. Nor are your skills as an animal trainer. What is, is your honesty.' Penni flicked back her hair and pointed an accusatory finger at Graham. 'Your ambition got the better of you and when you saw your opportunity, you took it. You stole Pudding from Edinburgh Zoo – and you faked a video purporting to show her safely returned to China, to cover your tracks!' She picked up her laptop and flipped it open triumphantly.

The screen showed a still from the video the Campbells had made last year, the one that 'proved' Pudding had returned to China. In the corner of the shot was the spindly house plant they'd used to make it look authentic.

'Let's take a closer look, shall we?' Penni zoomed in on the picture and scrolled right into the bottom corner. Just visible, sticking out from behind the leaves, was a plastic stake, with plant care instructions printed on it. On the top it read: *Dobbies Garden Centre, Edinburgh.*

'I think that's irrefutable evidence that the escaped panda from Edinburgh Zoo did not return to China, but in actual fact is living right here in Bumblescrape Street in Edinburgh. I'll have the animal welfare people on to you in a flash, as soon as I get the DNA results back from my panda fur testing.'

Callum gasped and stood up. 'You really are horrible. Pudding is not performing against her will. We adopted her and she lives with us.' Tears prickled at the corner of his eyes and Tabby's bottom lip wobbled.

'Did you ever think to ask *me* what I wanted?' Pudding said, drawing herself up to her best kind-but-stern stare. 'I am part of this family, Miss P, and I would like to stay here, thank you very much.' She put her big paws around Cal and Tabby and drew them in to a warm, fluffy bear hug.

Callum watched Penni while Pudding was talking and noticed how she was looking doubtfully back and forth between Pudding and Graham, whose mouth was now bulging with a double-chocolate-chip biscuit. But then she shook her head again.

'Clever to be able to throw your voice and eat at the same time, but you're not going to fool me, Graham Campbell. It's time for you all to face the music.'

CHAPTER 11
The Penni Drops

'Excuse me!' growled Pudding. She was fed up now. Cross about the whole situation – but mainly, cross with herself. She should have believed Callum from the start. The poor boy had really been trying to help all along. 'My voice is my own and I'll thank you to listen. Besides, if my old friend Gerald is to be believed, you're not exactly honest yourself. You'll do anything for a story. Isn't that right, Cal dear?'

Callum stepped forward and puffed out his chest. 'Penni, I mean Penelope, you're not some hotshot celebrity reporter. You're just an ordinary writer for an ordinary paper. When Pudding and I went to your office we asked the man at reception if Penni P worked there and he laughed, and now I understand why – you're faking being more important than you are. You even made up a silly name to sound fancier.'

Penni had turned beetroot red. Pudding knew Cal was probably feeling mean – but he kept going. *My brave boy*, she thought. Some things needed to be said.

'I heard you moaning about your boss – does he think you're ordinary too? Is that why you're trying to ruin our lives? You're the liar, not us.'

'Och, I think it's time for more biscuits,' said Dad with an exaggerated wink at Cal and Pudding. 'Excuse me a wee moment.' And he got up and left the room.

'Now listen to me, dear,' Pudding said sternly to Penni. 'I am indeed a living, breathing, talking panda and, what's more, I am part of this family.'

Penni looked around in confusion and Pudding realized why Penni was now looking a little alarmed. Graham had left the room while she, Pudding, was still talking!

Penelope had already worked out that Pudding was a real panda, but had apparently missed the bigger picture entirely. But come to think of it, perhaps Pudding had too. Being in a family was far more important than being in a movie – and no reporter was about to tear them apart.

'Now, you say you want what's best for me,' continued Pudding, 'and I'm telling you I want to stay. That's what is best. Do you really want to be responsible for tearing a happy family apart?'

Penni stared at Pudding. Her mouth was moving

but no sound was coming out. She looked around for Graham again, but he was gone and there was no getting around the actual truth.

'It talks,' she said. 'The panda . . . talks. It's . . . it's a talking panda.'

'*She*, please, Penni,' Pudding said.

Penni was gibbering now. 'The panda spoke to me. Nice panda. Nice talking panda.'

For once, the reporter had nothing else to say.

CHAPTER 12
Bear Necessities

Pudding turned to Cal and scooped him up in her soft paws. 'I am so, so sorry, Cal. I can't believe I got so carried away with being a movie star that I didn't take care of you and your sister. I forgot that I'm not the Star Attraction any more. I'm a nanny. I'm *your* nanny and that's the best job in the world.'

Graham came back into the room with a new packet of biscuits and a twinkle in his eye.

'Och, pet. Come and have a hug too,' said Pudding.

'I can't believe we're not going to Hollywood.' Dad sniffed and Mum took his hand.

'You're still a star to me, Daddy,' said Tabby with uncharacteristic sweetness as she slowly lifted the biscuits from his hand.

'Family is everything,' announced Pudding. 'I always wanted to be part of a real family, to be just like Mary Poppins. But I don't need to pretend to be her in a movie. I get to do it for real, right here. I don't need a black-and-white stretch limo, pure organic bamboo shipped from the Summer Palace, or my own personal shopper. I mean, whatever would I buy anyway? As long as we have a packet of these delicious biccies once in a while I'll be happy.'

They all had a huge family hug, wrapped in panda fur. But like any good nanny, Pudding seemed to have eyes in the back of her head, and saw Penni beginning to edge herself out of her seat.

'Oh no you don't, young lady. You sit yourself back down. We need to have a little talk.'

Penni did as she was told and slid back into the chair, biting her brand-new nails.

'Graham, would you mind putting on the kettle? I think Miss Peabody needs a cup of sweet tea. Just a spoonful of sugar.' Pudding sat down opposite Penni. 'Now, shall I call you Penelope, or Penni P?'

'Um, actually I think I like plain old Penny best. I'm sorry . . .' She started talking very quickly. 'Please believe me, I am sorry – I didn't realize you wanted to be here . . . I just assumed . . .' She looked down at her hands. 'You're right. Penni P is all fake – it's not me at all. A couple of days before I met you at the theatre I'd had a blazing row with my boss. He said I was a hopeless journalist and I'd never make it in the media industry. Then when I got that call about you, it felt like fate. Oh, I'm so ashamed. My friend

Amber did warn me that I shouldn't try to change myself, not like that. I wish I'd listened.'

Dad brought in the tea and Penny took it gratefully.

Cal was still scowling. 'You could've stopped any time,' he said. 'But you carried on, making up more and more lies. Making Dad and Pudding think their lives were going to change for the better, when in fact you were about to ruin everything.'

'No one likes a liar,' sang Tabby. 'Liar, liar, pants on fire!'

Mum popped Tabby on her lap. 'Don't forget, love, we've been keeping our secrets too. About Pudding. I told Callum the other day that secrets were a problem – and here we are.'

Suddenly there was a yell outside the living room. Spud Spiker had his son by the scruff of the neck – right outside the Campbells' living-room window – and was snarling at him. Mike looked really scared and Cal found himself feeling sorry for the boy, even if he had clearly been spying on their conversation with Penny. Spud realized the Campbells were watching and dropped his son like a stone.

'Ah see what yer up tae, wi' that great big beast in there. Dinnae think you'll be getting awa' wi' this for ever.' He waved his fist at them.

'Oh, for goodness' sake!' Pudding shut the window and whipped closed the curtains in his face. 'There. The Spikers have done their worst already! Let's just ignore them. Out of sight, out of mind.'

Cal found a weak smile start to spread over his face, even as Spud's muffled voice continued for a few moments. Maybe Pudding was right. Maybe they didn't need to worry any more. He turned to Penny. 'So, now that you know the truth about Pudding, what are you planning to do?'

Penny put down her tea, with a shaky hand. 'I can see now that Pudding is part of a loving family. I couldn't break that up.'

'You know,' said Pudding, 'not all news stories have to bring people down, or reveal horrible lies. Some great stories are happy. They lift people up, like a magic umbrella – and show them amazing things.'

'I could write a rave review about the show, if that's what you mean,' Penny said. 'It would be the least I could do!'

'I have a much better idea.' Pudding passed her an extra biscuit.

Six months later, Callum was in the kitchen with his mum, helping with a round of drinks for everyone.

'Here's your coffee, love,' said Mum, popping a mug down in front of Dad, who was working on a new comedy script to send to the BBC.

'How's it going?' asked Callum as he handed a glass of apple juice to Tabby, who was colouring in at the kitchen table and listening to music on her headphones.

'Ach, it's great, pet,' said Dad. 'I think they're going to love it! Especially the bit where Pudding dresses up as the Queen.'

'Right, off you go upstairs!' said Mum, handing Callum a tray, loaded with a mug of hot chocolate and two glasses of green juice – one spinach and apple, one bamboo – then turning to Dad. 'We'd better get started on lunch soon.'

Callum carefully carried the tray of drinks to the spare room, now converted into a studio. Pudding and Penny were sat in their usual places in front of the computer, laughing. They were concentrating hard and didn't notice the door opening. Pudding was pointing at something on the screen, as Penny worked her editing magic on their super-successful vlog.

'Smoothie delivery!' said Callum.

Pudding and Penny removed their headsets and spun around in their fancy office chairs. 'Marvellous!' Pudding said, slurping down half of her bamboo juice in one.

Penny pressed a few buttons on the studio keyboard and smiled warmly at her co-host. 'All done. The latest edition of *A Pudding for a Penny* is uploaded.'

'Even more marvellous! That interview you did with David Tennant is practically perfect. Especially when Gerald brought in Minnie the meerkat and they did that song-and-dance routine together. I bet it'll go viral!'

'Och, he's a lovely man.' She drank more of her juice. 'I've been thinking . . .'

Pudding put her head in her paws. 'Penny, you worry me when you get ideas in your head.' They shared a sisterly chuckle.

'No, seriously – we've done a lot of movie reviews and interviews now and I think it's time to take our little show a bit further afield.' Penny brushed her mousey-brown fringe out of her eyes. Callum's stomach lurched.

'You don't mean Hollywood, do you?' he said, worried.

Dad poked his head around the door. 'Did someone say Hollywood?'

Pudding looked up from her bamboo juice and grimaced.

'Oh no,' said Penny. 'I was thinking much closer to home – I'm a proud Scot, after all. How about we start at Holyrood, here in Edinburgh? I think that could be—'

Pudding looked at Dad and Dad looked at Cal, and they all laughed as they finished Penny's sentence.

PRACTICALLY PERFECT IN EVERY WAY!

Acknowledgements

Special thanks to Rachel, Barry, Laura, Elinor and Esther, the team at Chicken House, for accommodating more of my madcap ideas, and Emma Read for helping me knock this tale into a neat panda shape. Vikki Anderson, who had the original brainwave for a panda story, thank you for such an excellent idea to build and springboard off. I love working with you all.

Big thanks also to my agent Jodie Hodges and the team at United Agents, who do so much for me, often silently behind the scenes and without any fuss. Grateful to have you in my corner when navigating the wild publishing waters!

Hellos and thank yous to my dad (Pops) . . . my family and good friends for your continued support, love and encouragement; and to my nieces (the three naughty ones), Iris, Rose and Dora; and to the other delightful little people in my life, Benedict, Clara and JJ.

You are all AMAZING, and this is for you.

MILTON THE MIGHTY by EMMA READ
Illustrated by ALEX G GRIFFITHS

When spider Milton discovers he's been branded deadly, he fears for his life and his species. Alongside his buddies, big hairy Ralph and daddy-long-legs Audrey, he decides to clear his name. But to succeed, Milton must befriend his house human, Zoe. Is Milton mighty enough to achieve the impossible?

'. . . a charming and thoughtful read.'
THE SCOTSMAN

Paperback, ISBN 978-1-911490-81-4, £6.99 • ebook, ISBN 978-1-912626-31-1, £6.99

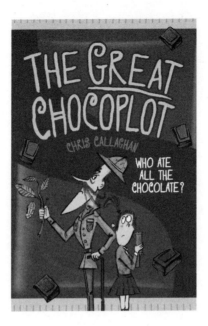

THE GREAT CHOCOPLOT by CHRIS CALLAGHAN

It's the end of chocolate – for good! A chocolate mystery . . . At least that's what they're saying on TV. Jelly and her gran are gobsmacked – they love a Blocka Choca bar or two. But then a train of clues leads back to a posh chocolate shop in town owned by the distinctly bitter Garibaldi Chocolati. Is it really the chocopocalypse, or a chocoplot to be cracked?

'With an excellent cast of characters, laugh-out-loud moments, and witty and sharp observations, this is a great choice for fans of Dahl and Walliams.'
THE GUARDIAN

Paperback, ISBN 978-1-910002-51-3, £6.99 • ebook, ISBN 978 -1-910655-57-3, £6.99

GRANNY MAGIC by ELKA EVALDS
Illustrated by TEEMU JUHANI

Will's beloved granny made cakes and knitted itchy jumpers – that's what he thought. But when she passes away and dodgy Jasper Fitchet moves in to their village, dark magic begins to unravel in Knittington. Can Will and his gran's old craft group tie Fitchet in knots? With the help of her old motorbike and a flock of magical sheep, they might just do it . . . so long as they don't drop a stitch.

'This joyous celebration of spinning and spells features motorbike stunts and gold-fleeced sheep.'
THE GUARDIAN

Paperback, ISBN 978-1-912626-19-9, £6.99 • ebook, ISBN 978-1-912626-65-6, £6.99